DR DEBB

MR I
DON'T
KNOW

MR I DON'T KNOW

SISTER

DAD

MOM

BROTHER

CHARLES

DOG

ALBERT

HOWARD

DR DEBBIE OBATOKI

MR I DON'T KNOW

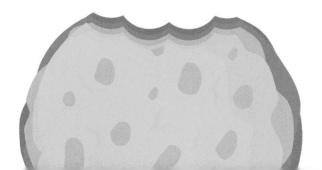

Albert smiled as his head popped up from his homework. "*That's what I need*," he said. Smells of roasted oat took form in his mind, and his mouth began to water as he scurried down the stairs and into the pantry. "*First the treat, then the milk*," he said, smiling an even deeper, more satisfied smile.

He reached up to the high shelf and there his fingers found the lid of a cookie jar which he tossed aside. Then Albert paused. Just for a moment, he closed his eyes and waited... There it was, that familiar smell. It settled down from above, that same smell that filled the house each time Albert's mum baked his most favourite of treats, the soft, sweet, salty, chewy... Anzac biscuits.

SUGAR

RICE

COOKIES

He tried to savour the moment, but the desire was more than he could bear. He stretched up onto the tips of his toes and reached his fingers down into the jar. *"What? No!"* he shouted, twisting his wrist this way and that, searching for what his heart and stomach had come to expect. But there was not even so much as a crumb. Only an oily residue remained to mock him.

Albert stared at his empty hands. *"Unbelievable,"* he said, shaking his head and sounding much more like his dad than he would ever come to realize.

"How can this be? This cannot be! She baked them only three days ago."

COOKIES

"*Mum!*" he screamed toward the kitchen. Surely, she would know where the biscuits had gone; who the offender was that had so hatefully stolen his long-sought joy. Maybe she would even have more Anzac biscuits hidden away somewhere. She knew how he loved them so. A smile began to form, but fell away. There was no answer.

"*Mum!*" he cried again, this time toward the stairs. But again, there was no reply.
"*Mum!*" he called again, now rounding into the kitchen.

"*Yes, Albert?*" came his mum's voice. Beyond the sliding glass doors, she sat busied beside a bucket of washed clothes.
Struggling to hold back his tears, Albert yanked the sliding glass door aside and had not yet stepped one foot onto the porch before he blurted out, "*Mum, look!*" and thrust forth the empty jar.

"*Oh, dear,*" she said. "*Empty.*"

"**W**ho has done it?" Albert said. "Who has finished the whole jar without me?"

Albert's mum nodded understandingly. "*Call your siblings,*" she said. "*We will get to the bottom of this.*"

"Sophie! Jack!" Albert shouted, sliding back across the smooth kitchen floor. *"Come quick! Mum's furious and you're both in terrible trouble!"*

A moment later, Jack came sliding down the staircase rail nearly crashing into Albert, who stood, arms crossed, at the bottom. Sophie was right behind. Both of Albert's older siblings wore scowls, but they always looked unhappy.

"What is it, Squeal?" Sophie asked, her scowl deepening as she and Jack stepped slowly closer to Albert.

Albert didn't much like that nickname, but he stood his ground. For once, armed with the knowledge that it was they who would be getting in trouble.

"*I*f Mum's so mad at us, why didn't she call us herself?" Jack asked, now standing so close that Albert could smell the sharp odour of cheese puffs on his breath. When Albert didn't answer, his siblings reached their hands out to grab him...

"*Out here, you guys,*" called Albert's mum from the patio, not sounding nearly as upset as Albert would have liked. But he appreciated her timing.

When they reached the patio, Albert's mum scanned over the three of them guardedly. Oh no, Albert swallowed. She's using her powers. As a young child, Albert used to wonder how his mum always knew what he had gotten up to at school, like she had pairs of eyes positioned everywhere he would go. He had concluded, however, and still believes, that she has the ability to read minds. He squinted his eyes, trying to block out her searching stare, but here again he was saved.

"*Sophie, Jack*," his mum began, "*Who finished the Anzac biscuits?*"

"*Which Anzac biscuits?*" Sophie asked.
Albert huffed, drawing a sharp elbow from his
sister and an even sharper stare from his mum.
"The ones I made a few days ago," his mum
continued.

"*I don't know,*" Sophie said.
Albert's mum stared at her daughter for a moment.
"*I see,*" she said, then turned her glance on Jack,
who put his hands up over his face, staring out
between fingers.
"*I don't know. I don't know,*" Jack squeaked before
his mum could speak.

"*Hmm,*" considered Albert's mum knitting her eyes
and turning them toward Albert. "*And what about
you?*"

Me! Albert thought, looking back in horror. How
could I be blamed, I was the one who discovered
them gone. "I don't know," he finally said, taking
a step backward. But to his surprise, his mum did
the same and a look of fear came over her eyes.

COOKIES

"*Not him again,*" his mum said.

"*Not who again?*" asked Albert.

"*Honey!*" called Albert's mum. "*Come quick! He's come back!*"

"*Who's come back?*" asked Albert, and he and his two siblings shared worried glances.

Albert's dad walked into the patio. "*What's this? Someone's come back?*"

"*Yes!*" said Albert's mum. "*I had hoped we were rid of him, but he's returned and stolen all the biscuits.*"

"*You know who stole the biscuits?*" asked Albert, not sure whether he was more confused, scared, or upset that she hadn't yet revealed the villain.

"*Yes, of course, I know,*" she said. "*You've just told me. You have all told me. Now we have only to find him.*"

"*Find him? Find who?*" Sophie asked. "*We haven't told you who stole the biscuits. When you asked, I've only said 'I don't know.'*"

"*You see, Honey?*" Albert's mum said to his dad. "*He's returned... Mr. I Don't Know.*"

"*Mr. I Don't Know?*" they all asked in unison.

"*That's right,*" their mum said, addressing the trio of siblings.
"*Ever since you three could talk, a person named "I Don't Know" has been sneaking into our house, stealing food, making messes, and breaking things. No matter where we've lived, he has always followed, and now he's had the nerve to eat the last of our beloved Anzac biscuits! The problem is, we can never catch him. I've never even seen him. I've only heard about him from the three of you. But enough is enough! Please tell Mr. I Don't Know to present himself for questioning.*"

A moment of the deepest silence passed, then everyone burst into laughter. Everyone except Mum. Albert looked at her and timidly said, "*But Mum, there is no such person.*"

"*Then who ate the biscuits?*" she replied flatly. Albert was silent for a moment, then, after glancing at his siblings, he took the risk. "*I don't know,*" he said, and everyone began laughing again. This time, for a moment, even their mum bore a reluctant smile. She cleared her throat, and Albert's dad stopped laughing immediately.

"*Alright, we've had our fun,*" Albert's dad said. "*In all seriousness, who ate the biscuits?*"

"*Well...*" Jack began. "*It had to be one of us, Dad.*"

As if released by Jack's words, Sophie stepped forward. "*I ate five Monday after school,*" she said with confidence, but shrank back from her words. "*Ellie was over. But we left quite a few.*"
"*And I had a couple,*" Jack said.
Albert smiled. Now they had it coming.
"*A couple?*" Dad asked, his eyebrows raising high on his forehead.

"*M*aybe six?" Jack corrected, "*...and another six for my basketball mate. He came home with me because his mum was running late. I had nothing else to offer him!*"

Jack hung his head. "*Sorry guys. We didn't eat the last of them, though.*"

All eyes turned to Albert.

"*Me? I didn't eat any.*"
"*Albert...*" Eyebrows rose again. This time, his mum's. "*A few nights ago, I heard the piddle paddle of tiny feet scurrying down the stairs and into the pantry,*" she said.

Albert smiled and looked down toward his feet. "*I only took two...*"
"*Albert...*"
"*...each time.*"

"*Well, it seems we have found our Mr. I Don't Know, after all,*" Albert's mum said. "*Let's do the math, shall we? I made twenty-six biscuits, and I know we each had one straight after, right? That's five.*"

Albert was not a lover of math, and turned his head from the question, hoping his mum would engage someone else.

"*Sophie took five,*" his mum continued, "*and Jack had twelve. Now we're at twenty-two. Add Albert's four and you've got twenty-six. Can we now understand why the biscuits are all gone?*"

Everyone nodded, including Albert's dad who had made himself comfortable on the lounge chair next to his wife and snapped to attention with an "Oh, yes, yes!" at her glance.

"*We need to stop blaming everything on Mr. I Don't Know,*" Albert's mum continued. "*When we take ownership of our actions, it helps us find solutions more easily. We save valuable time and don't have to do unnecessary math.*" She winked at Albert. "*Put the jar back in the pantry, Albert. I will make more biscuits tomorrow.*"

Albert smiled and did as he was told, disappointed that there hadn't been any backup biscuits, but happy that there would be more soon.

* * *

From that day on, everyone in Albert's house took responsibility for their own actions, and Albert didn't mind holding his siblings (and occasionally his dad) accountable. Family life became easier and easier, and complicated situations were resolved without fear or delay by using good communication. And best of all, Mr. I Don't Know left them and their biscuits alone.

* * *

THE END

To my late mother, *Ime Ernest Frank*, who made family life dynamic, fun and memorable.

As an early childhood educator, she encouraged parents to create a home environment kids could grow and thrive in because family life is important to the mental health stability of every child.

First paperback edition 9798747147331

Book design by R Graphic Studio
Illustrations by Colorfuel Studio

ISBN 9798747147331 (paperback)

www.theroundcubeink.com

SISTER

DAD

MOM

BROTHER

CHARLES

ALBERT

DOG

HOWARD

MR I DON'T KNOW

He comes and goes, yet nobody sees him.
His face and his ways are anyone's guess.
But Albert's craving shall reveal the
mischief-maker's familiar identity.

Mr I Don't Know strikes again.

Made in the USA
Middletown, DE
28 May 2021